A Girl Called Mary

Copyright ©2019 G D Waters

A Girl Called Mary

The story of fossil hunter Mary Anning

G.D. WATERS

A long time ago,
In a town by the sea

A baby was born,
And her name was Mary.

From that moment on,
Young Mary was changed
Was it the lightning?
That would be strange!

As Mary grew up,
Her family were poor,
So she worked selling shells
That she found on the shore.

Mary searched the beaches,
With her dad and brother Joe
There were treasures to be found
Amongst the pebbles below.

The objects they discovered,
Looked like shells and bones
Parts of ancient sea creatures
Turned into solid stone!

Today we call them fossils,
These clues from long ago

Were there others to be found?
Mary wanted to know...

One day the children
had a bit of a shock
A strange looking head
Peeking out of a rock!

Mary was excited!
What could it be?
A dragon or monster
With lots of sharp teeth?

News of the discovery
Spread far and wide!
What might it have looked like
When it was alive?

The fossil was sold,
And Mary was glad.
She could now help her family
With the money she had!

Mary knew more fossils
Were hidden on the beach
Was a new, exciting life
Almost within reach?

For months in the rain
She searched cliffs and rocks
Mary wasn't going to quit
Just because of wet socks!

Her next find was amazing!
Mary felt proud
A long-necked sea monster
It drew a huge crowd

Sea Monster

The people in town,
Couldn't believe their eyes!
Some said it wasn't real
That the fossil was a lie!

But they were very real,
The bones she had uncovered

A giant plesiosaur
The first to be discovered!

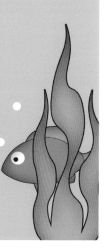

In Mary's home town,
They all knew her name
But away from the seaside
It wasn't the same...

The next fossil she found,
left Mary confused
The inside was rough
The outside was smooth!

?

Fish scales in the fossil
Gave Mary a clue!
The funny looking stone
was ichthyosaur poo!

Mary showed the world,
Just what girls can do
Boy OR girl, it doesn't matter
You can do science too!

Today Mary's creatures
Are displayed for all to see.
The greatest fossil hunter
The world has ever seen!

Ichthyosaur found by
Mary Anning

The End

About the Author

G.D. Waters lives on the south coast of England with her husband. She works in a museum where there are lots of fossils, including some found in Mary Anning's home town, Lyme Regis.

Printed in Great Britain
by Amazon